The Gamma Girls of Chagrin Falls

Lillie and Rose

Written by Janet Kuivila

Illustrated by Jane McKelvey

ISBN: 1-929774-18-4

Cover and Layout by Francine Smith
Illustrations by Jane McKelvey
Graphic Art by Gabe Minchow

Submit all requests for reprinting to:
Greenleaf Book Group LLC
8227 East Washington Street, #2
Chagrin Falls, OH 44023

www.greenleafbookgroup.com

Published in the United States by
Cats Ink., Cleveland, Ohio.

For Mrs. Mansager, my third grade
teacher in California, who always told me
I would write a book someday. – jlk

To my creative muse. – jm

The author wishes to express heartfelt
gratitude to editors Joyce L. Hoebing
and John S. Graham for their guidance,
feedback, patience and support, and to
her mom for finding all the typos.

A percentage of the proceeds from the sale of this book will be donated to Geauga Humane Society's Rescue Village.

For further information about this organization, readers can contact:

Rescue Village
15463 Chillicothe Road
Russell Township, Ohio
Phone: 440-338-4819
Email: rvshelter@alltel.net

rescue
village

TABLE OF CONTENTS

Part I: Lillie of the Valley

Chapter 1: Fire! .1
Chapter 2: What to Take 5
Chapter 3: Waiting and Wondering 15
Chapter 4: One Last Look 22
Chapter 5: A New Life 31

Part II: Lillie and Rose of the Valley

Chapter 6: A Friend! 38
Chapter 7: Off to School 45
Chapter 8: Meeting New People 53
Chapter 9: Alpha, Beta, Gamma 59
Chapter l0: A Fairy Garden 66
Chapter 11: Sammy's Gone! 75
Chapter 12: The Secret Door 80
Chapter 13: The Silver Ring 87
Chapter 14: A Gamma Plan 92
Chapter 15: Six Little Surprises! 98

What's a Gamma Girl?

"This girl isn't easily labeled... We'll call her a gamma, the third letter of the Greek alphabet... They are careful listeners, easy to talk to and laugh with."

– Laura Sessions Stepp, 'Alpha Girl: In Middle School, Learning to Handle the ABC's of Power.' Washington Post, February 23, 2002.

❧   ❧   ❧

"They're not mean. They like their parents. They're smart, confident and think popularity is overrated... Kids who may not be 'popular' but aren't losers either."

– Susannah Meadows, 'Meet the Gamma Girls,' Newsweek, June 3, 2002.

Part One:
Lillie of the Valley

Fire!

"Wake up," Lillie Jecmen's mother said. Her voice was somewhere between a whisper and a question. She gently rubbed her daughter's arm.

But Lillie was already awake. She had never really fallen asleep. She just kind of lay on her back, staring up at the dark ceiling. There was no way she was going to fall asleep, no matter how tired she was. How could anyone sleep?

"Wake up," her mother repeated quietly.

"I'm awake, Mom." Lillie had her

mother's brownish-blondish hair and her father's large brown eyes. But right now she felt completely gray.

It was probably around midnight in Jerome Prairie Valley, which was nestled in the southern part of Oregon. Lillie wondered what the other side of the mountain looked like right now, the side she couldn't see from her bedroom window. The side that was on fire.

She heard about the forest fire on TV every day and saw the bright red and orange pictures of the fire in the newspaper every evening. Homes, barns, trees, animals-all gone. She wondered what that might feel like.

"Well, then, it's time to get up, sweetie," her mother said.

"Right. I'll be right there."

Lillie knew that the raging fire was just over the mountain. Her family had been on a twenty-four hour evacuation notice, which meant they could be told to leave at any time of day or night. Now the dreaded notice had come. It was time to pack, time to go, time to escape the approaching flames.

FIRE!

The TV news called it the worst fire ever; it had gobbled up over half a million acres of the Kalmiopsis Wilderness area. It had been burning for a month, but always on the other side of the mountain.

However, for the last several days, the smoke would rise over the ridge like root beer foam, then spill over the crests, creeping toward the valley-toward Jerome Prairie Valley-until it was blanketed by the dense, heavy billows. Lately, the air was so thick that you could taste the soot and ash.

But at night, a breeze swept through, breaking up the smoke and pushing it back over the ridge. The smoke took on an eerie orange glow in the moonlight, and you could see it roiling, just waiting. Until daylight came again, the thick cloud hovered and simmered over the mountaintops, waiting to settle back into the valley.

It became harder to breathe. Lillie's eyes burned constantly, and her throat and lungs felt sore. The hanging cloud of smoke was a daily reminder of what was going on just out of sight. But as bad as the smoke was, Lillie preferred it to any fire.

Entire towns had to pack up and leave every day as the fire burned closer and closer. A high school gym, located behind a natural firebreak ten miles away, was housing families from Lillie's community until they were able to return to the site of their previous lives, if that was possible.

The TV news was filled with stories and images of these families, looking down at the ground where their homes had once been. They cried and shouted. What were they thinking of right then? Lillie wondered.

Lillie gathered up the duffel bag she had packed the day before and headed for the truck. Her dad told her that she should choose things that she would really miss if they were gone, and that everything would have to fit into her one bag. That included clothes.

2

What to Take?

Lillie had packed for vacations before, but this was different. She had to have room for clothes, books, favorite stuffed animals, pictures of her friends, and other little things she had collected over the years.

She had a rock and shell collection from their frequent trips to the coast. She had little glass bottles filled with sand from different places on the Oregon coast they had visited, like the dunes around Bandon and the beaches of Brookings and Newport.

She also put a scoop of soil from their hazelnut orchard into a tiny vial the size of her thumb, just in case she needed to remember it.

There were a lot of things she didn't pack. There were things she would be able to replace someday, like her basketball and some of her toys. There were things that took up too much space, like her giant stuffed tiger that she won at the county fair the year before. There were things that she just decided to leave behind, like her puzzles and board games. These were big decisions for a nine-year-old girl.

Her brothers were running around like little mice. They hadn't done much packing, and now only had thirty minutes before they had to leave. They didn't really believe that they were going to lose anything. They seemed to think that everything would be OK.

Nelson was still a little kid, only six

years old. He was always an active and curious guy, and one who worried- always asking if everything was OK, or if anything was going to get hurt. That's just the kind of boy he was.

Carter, the oldest of the three, acted a lot like Dad. He was twelve years old, but he seemed older. Many boys that Lillie knew who were twelve were always getting into trouble. Like taking joyrides in tractors or scaring cows into stampeding through cornfields. One of Carter's classmates got caught breaking into Old Lady Hoebing's house.

He was trying to steal one of her famous blackberry pies. She nearly shot him for being a burglar, until she saw he was only a kid.

But Carter was different. He was quiet,

a thinker, like Dad. He did what he was told, and he didn't hassle Lillie, even when she called him "Corky". But he was still an older brother and liked to boss her around and argue with her. The biggest problem with having an argument with an older brother like Carter was that he was usually right. He almost always won arguments with her.

Lillie passed her brothers in the hallway, shaking her head. Despite how smart they were, her brothers didn't like change. They thought that if the sheriff told them to leave, all they had to do was leave, like they did at the fire drills at school. Then they would come back and everything would be fine. In some ways, Lillie wished she thought like that. She wondered if she thought too hard for a nine-year-old.

Lillie stepped out the front door. Dad was busy packing what he could into the bed of their truck. He had already packed a lot of it the day before, but he saved some things for the last minute.

They might have been able to pack more things if they hadn't sold their older, smaller truck to pay for property taxes. Lillie remembered watching it go-she remembered how it smelled inside, a little sweet and a little spicy, like unripe blackberries. The truck they kept was bigger, but it was also newer, and it smelled more like gasoline and air freshener.

The farm hadn't been doing well over the last few years. Dad said it seemed like there were too many people trying to sell hazelnuts all at once. And her mom's medical practice was getting slower every year since Nelson had been born. Something to do with the jobs in southern Oregon being scarce and people moving away.

"Could you give me a hand with this, Lillie-belle?" Dad said, holding a group of branches strapped together.

"Frank," came her mother's voice from behind her. "You can't take those, there isn't going to be room."

"I have to take these, Dorothy," her dad said back. "They're cut from our best trees. We're going to have to replant when the..." he started to say something, then he stopped. "When we get back."

Not even her dad could say the word on

everyone's mind. *Fire* is what he was going to say. *When the Fire destroys everything we own.* Lillie tried not to look as upset as she felt. After all, she had everything she needed in her duffel bag.

"You can't replant our hazelnut trees, Frank," Mom said. "You know that. It'll take at least eight years before we can get anything out of them."

"That's no reason to give up."

Mom sighed and went back into the house.

"Did anyone find Sammy Calico?" Lillie called after her mom.

"No, sweetie," was the reply from inside the house.

Sammy, their calico cat, had left the day before. Lillie saw him last when she was busy packing. He must have sensed that something was wrong and decided he didn't want to hang around. Nelson was the first to notice he was missing.

He had always been an independent cat, disappearing for days at a time. He could be sweet, sitting on the couch with Lillie to have his tummy rubbed. But he liked to roam around, too.

Carter called him "the King" because he liked to have a lot of land to survey as his little kingdom. Sometimes he sat at the top of the biggest hazelnut tree, just watching everything going on beneath him. Other times he crouched down under the tall grasses in the hay field, unaware that others could see him spying on the field mice.

Lillie helped her dad get everything they could into the truck. She helped him search around the garage and the storage barn. There wasn't much left that they could save. There was no way they were going to move the heavy-duty table-saw that Dad used for his woodworking business, which was his side job when the hazelnuts weren't in season. When the delivery people brought it in, they had to use a small crane. Then her dad bolted it to the floor. It wasn't going anywhere.

When everyone was in the truck- Lillie, her mom, her dad, her two brothers- and everything they could fit, they slowly backed away from the farmhouse, then turned and drove down the long, gravel driveway to Woodland Park Road.

Lillie looked hard at her house, brightly lit by the glow of the large, full moon. She tried to etch it into her memory. She stared toward the giant sycamore tree that she had fallen out of and broken her ankle, at the stream running through the blueberry field where she caught her first fish, and to the field where they cut mazes through the uncut hay every autumn.

She looked up to see the starry night sky being covered over with a brown foggy smoke. The wind wasn't blowing the smoke away anymore. It had shifted and now it was all coming over the mountain, the thick bank of dirty air-and everything it brought with it- toward their farm. The fire wasn't far away.

Oh, no! Lillie suddenly thought of something she had forgotten to pack. It was some-thing small, but still important, that she shouldn't have forgotten. It was the little metal ring that she bought at a garage sale a couple of years ago, when she was younger, maybe six or seven. It was silver colored with six hollow hearts.

There had been a girl at the sale about her age who sat behind her mother in the shadows of the front patio. The girl had stringy red hair and freckles and didn't look happy. Lillie remembered digging into her pocket for a nickel and handing it to the mother. The girl looked up briefly at Lillie, then looked back down at her feet.

Now, Lillie really wanted that ring. She wanted to scream and cry for her dad to stop so she could run to her room and get it from her dresser drawer. But she didn't say anything. She knew that the time for her to pack had passed. And now they were on their way to safety.

When the truck got to the main road, there were vehicles with flashing lights, and people in black and yellow uniforms directing traffic. Lillie held on to her duffel bag tightly and tried not to think of Sammy. No one said anything as they drove along the highway, in a procession with an endless line of taillights and safety cones.

Lillie laid her head against the window and stared out into the dark forest that surrounded the highway.

3

Waiting and Wondering

Lillie could picture herself climbing
into their huge sycamore tree, high
where the branches came to a gentle ar
comfortable V. It was high enough so th
her brother Nelson couldn't bother he
And even though her brother Carter coul
have climbed that far, he usually didn't. U
there, the branches didn't quite fit togethe
and the leaves weren't so thick, so it gave
her a spectacular view of the mountains.

She could see them perfectly, as though viewing through a telescope. Every day was a diferent picture. In the fall, the mountains wer speckled with gold and orange aspen and oak, among the evergreen Douglas Fir and Ponderosa Pine. Winter brought a sprinklig of snow like powdered sugar, thick on the tops of the mountains with just a gentle duing on the lower parts.

She first saw the smoke through that syamore telescope. That was just two weks ago, but it seemed like months, like a wole season had gone by and changed the cor of the landscape all by itself.

   ❧   ❧   ❧

It seemed like forever until they got to e high school. They had to park along the arrow street because the school's parking lot was already packed.

Lillie looked at her two watches. One was yellow with a pink horse on the dial, and the other was silver with a digital dial. The yellow one said it was around 2:30, and the silver one said it was exactly 2:32 A.M.

Lillie walked with her family to the gym, which buzzed with a kind of quiet anxiety. It seemed like the whole valley had been emptied right into there. People were setting up their air mattresses and cots and sleeping bags. Lillie thought she wasn't going to get any sleep. She sat on the floor looking at her shoes and tried to think of happier things.

Lillie's favorite season was spring, when the color of newness and freshness replaced the bleached look of winter, outshining the dark green pines and covering up the bare, splotchy branches of the madronas. Spring was cool and wet and a muddy kind of comfortable.

But late summer in the valley was no one's favorite time of year, not even with school being out. It was hot, and people were always restless. Summer meant that the rain stopped, and the brush that grew in the wild spring rains had dried up into kindling. It was August and the valley was stuck in the middle of the yearly drought, when mud turned to dust and everything slowed down. Everything except for the forest fires.

Living in the valley meant living with this danger every summer. Even Lillie knew that. And every once in a while someone in southern Oregon lost their home. Usually it was just one or two families, but this year it was entire towns.

The air was already so hot during the day that Lillie felt like she wasn't getting enough oxygen; when she was in the sun, her skin felt like an empty skillet on the stove. But now with the fires, the air was filled with something besides the August heat, besides smoke and soot. It was a mixture of desperation and hope, and she could see it on the faces of the people around her in the gym. It happened at night as well as during the day.

She recognized a lot of the kids there, most of whom were sleepy or sniffling or huddled together with their families. Few of them looked like they wanted to be noticed.

There was her friend Alyssa from her

school, but she looked like she was asleep. There was Phillip, the kid no one seemed to like because he threw rocks at everyone. He never really said much. There was C.J., who always raised her hand when the teacher asked a question. That was annoying. It wasn't just that she always raised her hand, it was that she practically levitated out of her seat trying to make her hand higher than anyone else's.

Lillie waved. C.J. waved back with a meek hand. No one wanted to be recognized.

Dad was setting up the sleeping bags on one part of the gym floor. Nelson looked up at him and said, "Dad, what will happen to the animals?"

"Well," Dad said as he rolled out a sleeping bag. "I opened up the chicken coop and I left the fences open for the goats and the cows. I'm sure they've gone by now. They'll have to take care of themselves for a bit. And Sammy's been gone a while now. He's safe somewhere."

Lillie could tell that was little comfort to her younger brother. They all missed Sammy

Calico, even Dad, who had muttered, "Dumb cat," more than once at the farm.

"Sammy wouldn't like it here," Lillie said. "There are too many people."

"He's OK," Carter said. "He's probably just curled up somewhere with a full belly."

Carter's words echoed in Lillie's head as they all stopped talking and tried to sleep in a room full of a hundred other people.

Past the strange silence of the gym, past the people coughing and murmuring in the quietest tones, they could hear the barking of dogs that had been left in cars in the parking lot outside. None of the pets understood what was going on any more than anyone else did.

🐾　　🐾　　🐾

Lillie slept badly that night, listening to people snoring and rolling around in their sleeping bags. Some thoughtless people had left their little radios on, trying to listen to any news about the fire. They could at least have put headphones on, Lillie thought.

"Hey, Corky," she whispered, tapping her older brother on the shoulder.

"What do you want, Lillie?" Carter said without moving.

"What's that smell? It's so familiar... I can't think of it, but I know it."

Carter was silent for a moment, inhaling. He rolled over and sat up on one arm to face her. "It's the wood floor," he said. "They put some kind of wax on it. It's what all gyms smell like."

Lillie thought about that. He could be right. "I wonder if our old school gym burned down," she said.

"You think of the weirdest stuff, Lillie." He rolled back over. "I'm going to pretend to sleep now, so don't bother me," he said.

"Then I'm just going to pretend to bug you."

"Whatever."

Lillie sat up. The lights in the ceiling weren't all the way on, but it wasn't exactly dark. She didn't like sleeping with that much light. She needed it to be really dark and really quiet in order to get to sleep. Otherwise, it sometimes took her hours before she fell asleep.

4

One Last Look

About a week later, at about 7:00, or 7:02 A.M., depending on which watch Lillie looked at, her dad woke her up.

"We're going back now, Lillie-belle," he said quietly. "Roll up your sleeping bag and let's get moving."

She looked around and noticed a lot of people were gone already, maybe half. She took her sleeping bag and her duffel bag and followed Carter back to the truck. Her heart started to pound in her chest. What was waiting for them when they got back?

Everyone was unusually quiet on the drive back. They passed a few emergency vehicles, and at one point had to slow down for some reason that Lillie couldn't see. Lillie was aware of her breathing. Her heart now felt like it was shaking her whole body. She almost started to cry. There was too much for her to be worried about.

Almost like they passed into another world, they came around a corner to see a changed landscape. Lillie heard her mom gasp. Her dad said something she couldn't quite hear.

On either side of the highway, the damage was incredible. Where there used to be a forest, there was now blackened, steaming ground with charred remains of trees. Oddly, some tall trees were still standing, with just a few burned branches at the top.

Lillie recognized the smell of fireplaces mixed with some kind of pungent chemical. There were some areas where firefighters in yellow shirts and silver hardhats were walking around. She could see some of them in the distance in fields and on bare, darkened hillsides.

Lillie's mom rolled down her window. Immediately, they were all hit with the strong smell of wet ashes and old smoke.

"It smells like Aunt Lenore," Nelson said.

Mom stifled a laugh.

"The fire jumped right over the high-way," Dad said. "Look at that. The fire chief said it moved really fast. They'd never seen anything like it. Apparently, it's still burning east of here."

That didn't make Lillie feel any better. Her stomach was in a knot. Didn't anyone else feel anxious about what shape their house was going to be in?

They pulled off the highway onto Woodland Park Road, which led to their house. There used to be a row of pine trees on both sides of the road, then a small rise and some rocks. That's where the fence start-ed as it followed the road on either side.

But there was no fence. It had been burned away with the surrounding forest. Every once in a while along the road, there was a metal post sticking out of the ground. Dad had added those a few years ago to help support some of the weak wooden fence posts. He didn't really need to keep the fence up; the cows were kept in a pen on the other side of the property. At least, they used to be. The fence was just some kind of marker that let them know they owned that land.

Lillie knew as soon as she saw those metal posts sticking out of the ground that the house was gone. As the truck left the road and climbed up their driveway, the top of the house was supposed to be visible, then gradually the whole house would come into view.

But, of course, it wasn't there. She didn't really expect it to be there, but it was still a shock when it came. Not really a shock. It was more of a blow, like when she fell out of her sycamore tree and had the wind knocked out of her. Her lungs began to burn, but this time it was because she had stopped breathing. Lillie inhaled deeply.

She heard her mother gasp again.

There were a couple of firefighters walking around with large yellow canisters.

Dad stopped the truck. His voice suddenly got very low and very serious.

"Carter," he said without turning, "help me take a look around."

Carter got out of the truck quietly, and the two of them started checking things out. Mom helped little Nelson to the ground. Lillie got out, too. They walked over to where the house used to be. The brick chimney that went all the way to the roof had tumbled down so that it only stood up three or so feet. The bricks in the pile beneath it were blackened with soot.

In her mind, she could see the house as it stood-she knew where her room would have been in the space above the foundation. She started to head for that spot.

"Stay back, little girl," said one of the firefighters. "It's not safe there. Wait until we tell you it's safe."

Lillie nodded. She looked around at the horizon. With no trees around, it was easier to see the mountain ranges in the distance. She hadn't noticed it before, but they were surrounded on all sides by different mountaintops and rises. Her sycamore tree was gone, and in its place was the view of a grayish-green mountain peak.

She looked back at where the house used to be. Somewhere in that pile of burnt timbers and sooty bricks was her ring with the six hearts on it.

Dad was standing over where his shop used to be. The mammoth table saw, once the center of the shop, was now a charred and twisted blob of metal. Lillie walked over and hugged his waist.

"Are you OK, Dad?" she asked.

"Sweetie," he said, "this can all be replaced. We're all safe and healthy. That's what's important."

"The sadness we are all feeling will pass with time," Mom said.

The Jecmens lingered at the site of their home and farm a little longer, said their own silent prayers and goodbyes, and climbed back into the truck.

❀   ❀   ❀

On their way out, they stopped about a mile from home at the little corner store they used to walk to. Lillie had many good memories of spending her allowance money in the candy aisle. Today they needed a few supplies, but mostly just wanted to say goodbye to the friendly storeowners, Mr. and Mrs. Walter, who had been their neighbors for as long as she could remember.

Dad and Mr. Walter marveled at the path of the fire. The store had been right in the fire's path, but at the last minute the winds had shifted in a strange way and spared it. It wasn't that far from the Jecmen farm.

"Did the fire get you some?" Mr. Walter asked.

"It pretty much wiped us out," Dad said. "We used to have five hundred hazelnut trees. Now we have less than thirty."

Lillie half-listened to this conversation. She noticed a green dish on the ground just outside the front door.

"Do you have a cat?" Lillie asked Mrs. Walter.

"We sort of have a number of cats," she said. "Can't say we're their owners or anything. They're wild mostly. No tags or anything. That dish there is frequented by a friendly cat we like to call Sundae. Hey, do you guys need any pet food for the road?"

"No pets," Dad said.

Lillie wandered outside and looked around the bushes near the back delivery door. There were more dishes filled with the store's day-old food.

"Hey!" she heard from behind her in the truck. "Lillie! Come here!" It was Nelson.

In the back of the truck, curled up on one of the black plastic storage bags, was Sammy, looking like he had been sleeping on a king's silk pillow.

"Was he in the truck the whole time?" Nelson asked.

"No, doofus," Carter said. "We would have seen him."

Dad and Mr. Walter came outside.

"That's Sundae," he said. "He's been

coming to our store for almost a year. Eats everything we put out for him, especially the ice cream."

"No, that's *our* cat, Sammy!" said Lillie. "And he eats everything *we* put out for him!"

They all exchanged good-byes and good lucks, and the Walters handed the Jecmens a big bag of cat food for the very fat, very happy Sammy.

      🐾   🐾   🐾

A few days later, the Jecmens began the long drive across the country-over the Rockies, past the plains, across the Mississippi River and through the farmland of the Midwest. It was late September when they got to the Chagrin River Valley outside of Cleveland, Ohio.

The town in the valley was called Chagrin Falls. Chagrin Falls, Ohio. Lillie's new home.

5

A New Life

The Jecmen family had moved thousands of miles away. Lillie's mom had grown up in Ohio, and her family home was still there, empty and waiting.

"We're not going to have a lot of money for a while," Dad had said as they wearily unloaded the truck. "The farm back home is up for sale, but so far no one has had any interest in it. Mom's job at the clinic is just starting, so we're just going to have to live very frugally for awhile."

Nelson said, "What does *frugally* mean?"

"It means," said Carter, "that you're not going to get any new toys for a while."

That was fine with Lillie. She had lost a lot of things in the fire, but they didn't mean as much to her as she thought they might. Carter was angry with himself that he didn't save his Bob Feller autographed baseball, but like he said: "It's just stuff."

When Lillie first walked into their new house, she felt cold, still air. The house had two stories and it echoed like a church, especially up the stairs. It had belonged to her gramma, but no one had lived in it for about ten years. There were cobwebs hanging down from the ceiling, and there was a thick layer of dust over every surface.

"We'll be busy cleaning this place," Mom said.

Sammy made himself right at home on the stairs, joyfully rolling back and forth and covering himself with dust.

"There's no furniture here," said Nelson.

"That's OK," said Mom. "We have sleeping bags so we'll do indoor camping for awhile," she added, smiling wide for

Nelson's sake. She turned to Lillie. "Hey Lillie-belle. A lot of my old things are still in the barn. Why don't we go have a look around?"

"You kept all that stuff?" Dad said.

"It's not that I kept it," Mom said. "It's just that we never got around to tossing it out."

Mom led Lillie out to the barn, which was separate from the house but connected by a winding brick walk. The barn door was kept closed with a very rusty, very old padlock.

"I don't think anyone's been in here for years," Mom said, fishing some keys out of her pocket. She fiddled with a key in the lock. It opened with a reluctant grinding noise.

Lillie helped her slide the door open from left to right. It creaked and squealed like a piglet being chased.

"Hey, look!" Lillie cried.

Right in front, there was a very old bicycle. It was red with thick tires and little plastic streamers coming out of the handle-bars. Lillie never had a bicycle of her own, but she used to ride some of her friends' bikes around school back in Oregon.

"This is so amazing!" Lillie said. "Did this used to be yours?"

"It sure was!"

"I have to get some air in the tires. Where can I do that?" asked Lillie.

"I'll bet there's an old tire pump in here somewhere. Ah yes, here it is. Let's see if it works."

After some spray-on machine oil, it did work. And soon Lillie was riding around the long driveway that led from the barn to the house to the road. She decided to go for a ride around the neighborhood.

"Hey!" Mom called. "Don't you want to see what else is in the garage?"

"Later!" Lillie yelled back. This was the first time since the fire that she felt truly carefree.

Part Two:
Lillie and Rose
of the
Valley

6

A Friend!

It felt odd riding on the uneven, cracked bricks of Falls Road. The bike was making strange creaking and clicking noises, but it was holding together. It was also for someone maybe a little smaller than Lillie, like someone who was a couple years younger. She would have to ask her mom about it later.

Lillie checked out the other houses on her new street. They were nestled away deep in the woods, hidden away from the road. She was used to wide open spaces of pastures dotted with cows and horses and clumps of trees. These woods had a different smell and feel than the Oregon forests. She decided she liked both.

She rode around, noticing that the houses were a lot closer to each other than she was used to. Even though they were hidden by the trees, she wondered if it would make her feel closed-in, being so near the other families.

Mostly she looked up at all the trees. Some of them she recognized, but most of them were new to her, like the ones with the big, fat pointy leaves. Some were just starting to turn colors. They were still mostly green, but there was some yellow and even some orange and red.

She rode around some more and saw some kids playing ball in the street. They stopped to look at her. She waved. They kind of half-waved back. They didn't recognize her.

It didn't matter. Lillie had the sun on her face and she could fly faster than the wind, even on that little old bike.

She turned the corner onto Main Street and rode up a driveway that led to an open field. All of a sudden, she heard a metal screech and clunk. She felt her legs spinning with no resistance, and her bike began to slow down.

She looked at her feet. The chain had come off and was now just hanging there.

"Oh, great!" Lillie said aloud. She walked the bike into a driveway and leaned it against a tree.

"Hi," someone behind her said quietly.

But there wasn't anyone there, just a big line of bushes along the side of the road.

"You with the bike," the voice said again. It was a girl's voice.

"Who's there?" Lillie asked the bushes.

A girl about Lillie's age emerged from the bushes, looking down at the brick road, then at the bike, then at Lillie, then down again. She seemed shy.

"I'm Rose," she said softly. "Rose Williams."

Rose had a kind, pretty face and her bright, blue eyes sparkled. She wore a green sundress, with a row of hot air balloons flying across the front. On her feet were lavender tennis shoes with bright yellow socks. She had a straw hat in her hand. Her dark brown hair was very long and all over the place.

"My name's Lillie."

"Hey, that's funny," Rose said. "We're both flowers."

Rose looked down again. "Looks like you've got problems with your bike."

"The chain's broken," said Lillie.

"Nah, it's not broken. It's just fallen off. I could fix it for you," Rose said, putting one hand on her chin and scrunching up the hem of her dress with the other. "You know, if you want." Her voice was barely above a whisper.

"That's OK," Lillie said. "I can do it."

"You can?"

"Sure. I've never had a bike before, but it seems just like a rubber band."

Lillie sat down and pulled the chain up from the ground. It was greasy on her fingers. She wrapped it around the pedal wheel then pulled the small end around the gear on the back wheel. It was tight, but she managed it.

"See? Easy!" Lillie said. She wiped her hands on her pants.

"You're talented, Lillie."

"Yeah. I guess. But you could do it, too. Right?"

"Oh, sure I could. No problem. Well, that's not exactly true, I guess. I mean, no, not really. I would have no idea how to fix that, but I was gonna try."

Lillie started laughing. "You're a strange flower, Rose."

Then Rose started laughing, too.

"That's a weird looking bike," Rose

said. She put her straw hat on, which covered up almost all of her long dark hair.

"It's over thirty years old," Lillie said proudly. "It was my mom's when she was a little girl. Do you want to ride it?"

"I... I don't think so. It's kind of old, isn't it?"

"Come on, you can ride it. It's not going to fall apart. I mean, not anymore. You can ride it back to my house. We just moved in around the corner."

"I don't ride bikes. I mean, I've never had a bike."

"Come on! I'll hold the seat so you don't fall."

Rose reluctantly got on the bike and stood on the pedals while Lillie half-held, half-pushed her along. Rose looked terrified as she rattled along on the bricks, but Lillie kept her steady.

"So you're going to go to school here?" Rose asked as she tried to keep her balance. Her voice was shaking. "What grade are you in?"

"Fourth," Lillie replied.

"That's what grade I'm in!" Rose said. "But school's already started."

"I know," said Lillie. "School starts early here, in August. We started after Labor Day in September back in Oregon.

"It'll be okay. I moved here last year right after spring break. Maybe we can be friends."

"We already are friends, you strange flower!"

Rose smiled.

When they got back to Lillie's house, Rose's eyes got wide. "This is your house?" She sounded surprised. "No one's lived here for so long. Everyone says its haunted." She nearly fell off the bike when they came to a stop, but she regained her balance in time.

Lillie introduced Rose to everyone, but Rose was acting shy again and didn't say much. She pulled her hat down farther on her forehead.

Lillie wondered why her new friend was so shy around other people but not around her.

7

Off to School

Rose left for the weekend to visit her father, who lived in Cleveland. She wouldn't be back until the night before Lillie's first day of school on Monday.

Lillie still couldn't believe that fourth grade had already begun. It made her miss her friends back at her old school in Oregon. She wondered where they would be going to school now, since the old school had burned down. She wrote a couple of letters to them, but she hadn't gotten an answer.

They were probably busy cleaning up after the fire-if there was anything to clean up.

Nelson was afraid that he wouldn't make any new friends. At lunch on the day before their first day of school, he was very nervous.

"You're the only person I'm going to know," he said to Lillie. "Carter will be at a different school."

"You probably won't see much of Lillie," Mom said. "But this is part of the fun of going to new places. You get to make all kinds of new friends."

"That doesn't sound like much fun," Nelson complained.

"Don't worry about it so much," Carter said. "Kids like it if you just start talking to them. Just start talking to someone."

"You'll do fine, dear," Mom said.

"I'll look out for you," Lillie said. That

seemed to make Nelson feel better.

Lillie couldn't help feeling the same things that Nelson did. She was glad to have Rose as a friend, but if she went away to see her father in Cleveland every weekend, how could they do things together?

"It's so quiet here," Rose had said of Chagrin Falls. "I'm used to things going on in the big city. You know, people walking by, talking, driving, beeping. City noises. Here the wind is louder than the people."

"Are you serious?" Lillie said. "Because I think there's so much activity here. The houses are so close together you can see your neighbors through the trees. I'm used to it being really quiet, and being so far away from other people that you could shout your head off and no one would turn to look at you like you were crazy."

Rose had looked at her like she was crazy.

      🐾   🐾   🐾

Lillie found out that her new school had a tiger for a mascot. Shopping for new clothes at the mall, Lillie chose a yellow dress that had paw prints all over it, and tiger-striped tights. It made her think of her orange sweatshirt with the black outline of a tiger's face that she used to have. She had not chosen to save that from the fire.

The morning of their first day of school, Dad had to make sure that Lillie and her brothers took the right buses and remembered their room numbers. Fortunately, all the buses had a stop at the same place at the end of their driveway. Carter's bus came and went, and Lillie and Nelson waited for theirs.

Lillie patted Nelson on the head before they got on the bus. "Don't worry," she said. "Just think you're OK and you'll be OK."

"Sure, Lillie," he said. Then they got on the bus, waving to their dad as they left. They sat together on one of the bench seats.

Nelson leaned across the aisle and started talking to another boy who was his age. "Hi, my name's Nelson," he said with almost no fear. He quickly moved over to the seat with the other boy, leaving Lillie by herself. He had already found a friend and they hadn't been on the bus for more than ten seconds. She was happy for him.

It was hot that morning, even though it was September. "Indian Summer" her dad had called it. Lillie wore her tiger dress and tights on her first day of school. She sat on the bus, hoping someone would say hello, but no one did. She kept telling herself the same thing she told Nelson, *Just think you're OK and you'll be OK.*

She sat alone on the seat in the middle of the bus until a blond girl with headphones around her neck sat next to her. She had the most amazing hair Lillie had ever seen. It was neatly pulled back into a high ponytail, which hung in perfect ringlets all the way down her back. Lillie started to say something, but the blond girl started talking to someone else in the seat behind. She watched the girl's ringlets bounce up and down as the bus rattled along.

Lillie noticed that the blond girl-and all the other girls she had seen so far-was wearing short capri pants in autumn colors. She wondered if her tights looked like they might be capri pants. She looked around for Rose, but her friend wasn't on the bus.

The blond girl talked to the other girls the whole time. Lillie stared out the window, looking at the neighborhood. There were so many houses in Chagrin Falls! And Rose thought this was quiet!

The bus turned into the school. She got up from her seat and was jostled heavily by the other kids. It was a real traffic jam. She wasn't used to that. She got pushed this way and that until finally she almost fell down the steps at the front of the bus.

Now she felt like she was part of a stampede. The crowd pushed her through the school doors, down the hall and toward the lockers. She saw a group of girls hanging out in front of the classrooms. They all had on those same capri pants. And though their shirts were all different colors, they were basically the same shirt.

Lillie decided to go up to them. "Hi," she said.

"Hey," one of them said. "Nice dress."

Was she being nice or sarcastic? Lillie couldn't tell. The girl had that same long, blond hair in a high, bouncy ponytail, and she had those same headphones around her neck with the wire leading to a pack around her waist. Lillie made sure she wasn't the same girl who was on the bus. Nope. Curls, but no ringlets.

The other girls turned away from her, and walked down the hall. They were following the girl who gave Lillie the compliment, if it was indeed a compliment.

Where was Rose?

One of the capri pants girls came up to Lillie. "You're the new girl, aren't you?" she asked. It was the kind of question that didn't expect an answer. The other girls waited behind her.

"Yep," Lillie said. "This is my first day."

Suddenly, the girl on the bus with the ringlets stepped up. She put one hand on her hip and looked Lillie up and down. Then she spoke.

"A little tip, Miss New Girl. We don't wear dresses here."

"Hey," Lillie said suddenly. "What's your name?"

"You'll find out soon enough," she said with a big, fake smile. "Everybody knows who I am." Then she skipped and ran back to her friends, all of them laughing.

Lillie walked to her class alone.

8

Meeting New People

She managed to get through the first half of the day without making any major blunders, which was her goal. Everyone seemed friendly, but she didn't really get to know anyone.

It wasn't until lunchtime that Lillie saw Rose, wearing her hot-air balloon dress just like the first time they met.

Lillie was looking for a place to sit in the lunchroom when she saw Rose sitting at a table by herself.

"Hi Rose! Did you have a good time in

Cleveland?"

"I guess."

"Did you see the Rock & Roll Hall of Fame?"

"I've seen it before. We just stayed at my dad's house."

Lillie looked over at the lunchroom building. "I'm glad you're wearing a dress today."

"This is Indian Summer in Ohio. It's too hot to NOT wear a dress. This place doesn't have air conditioning."

"Who's that blond girl with the..." Lillie started to say.

Rose interrupted her. "That's Alexandria Winslow," she said flatly. "I know exactly who you mean. She makes a big production out of everything. She's never alone, if you'll notice," Rose said. "Even at the grocery store when she's with her mom, she's got a friend with her. She's always surrounded by other girls who look just like her."

"Aren't they all friends?"

"If you can call that being friends, I guess. Just watch, though. If Alexandria changes her hairstyle, all the other girls change theirs, too. Sometimes it takes a couple of days, but they all start to look like her. When I first came here last spring, she had shorter hair that she put in pigtails, and she wore dresses almost every day. Then one day she started putting her hair in a ponytail and wearing those little short pants."

"Capris," Lillie said.

"Whatever. And then the other girls started wearing them, too. Then they started using curlers to try to get the ringlets, but nobody can quite get those right. Alexandria's hair curls into them naturally. I don't know why they all try so hard to copy her. Maybe she threatened to not talk to them if they didn't."

Lillie looked back at the lunchroom. Alexandria and her friends were on the benches outside now, talking and drinking bottled water while their ponytails flipped back and forth.

"She's not so bad," Lillie said. "She's just an attention getter. You know, she likes to have everyone's attention, that's all."

"Well, she's got it," Rose said. "Just look at her."

"Nah. I'd rather see the school. I haven't seen the whole place yet."

"Let me show it to you."

The two girls got up, taking their trash over to the trashcans. There were some boys hanging around them. One of them, a pale, skinny boy who was taller than the others, had a shock of bright, red hair on top of his head. He squinted his eyes and smiled at Rose menacingly.

"Hey Rose, you're pretty," he said while clenching his teeth into a wide, fake smile.

Rose rolled her eyes at Lillie like she knew what was coming next.

Then the boy said, "Pretty ugly. AND full of hot air today, I see."

Rose stuck her tongue out at him as they walked by.

"Yeah," the boy said. "That makes you look better."

When they were far enough away, Lillie turned to face him and said, "You should leave your brain to science! Maybe they could find a cure for it!"

Then Lillie grabbed Rose's hand and they started running, laughing as they went. When they went around the corner by the gym, they stopped.

"Who was that boy?" Lillie asked.

"That's Johnnyrotten," Rose said. "He's a jerk. He's a total jerk."

"Is that really his name? Johnnyrotten?"

"No. It's Fairly or Farley or something. I don't remember. I call him Johnnyrotten because he's so rotten. I can't believe you said that to him."

Out of the corner of her eye, Lillie saw a big clump of kids coming toward them. It was a group of students coming back from lunch. One of them was Nelson.

"Hey Lillie. Hey Rose," he said.

"Hey," Lillie said. "What's going on?"

"I met a lot of people, Lillie. You were right. All I had to do was go up and talk to some kids. It was easy."

"Thanks," Lillie said. "But Carter's the one who told you that."

9

Alpha, Beta, Gamma

"Hey! New girl!" Lillie heard from behind her. It was one of the girls who followed Alexandria around. She was with a couple of girls who Lillie didn't recognize. "I heard you threw a rotten tomato at Johnny Farly by the trash can."

"Who says I did?" Lillie asked suspiciously. "I didn't throw a tomato at anyone."

"Alexandria says so," another one said. "I think it's so funny. I wish I had been there to see it."

"All I did was throw him an insult."

"I think you're in trouble."

Lillie started to protest again, but the other girls started giggling and then walked away. Lillie was very confused now.

Then Lillie saw Johnnyrotten across the parking lot. His red hair was bouncing on the top of his head like a bird flapping its wings. He looked at her, then he stared at her, then he glared at her. It seemed like he might come towards her, but he just turned around and headed toward the bus.

Apparently, word had gone around school about her little insult, and someone had blown it way out of proportion.

Lillie got on the bus and looked around. Nelson was chattering away with another boy in a seat near the front. Lillie smiled and walked past, and plunked down in the first open seat near the back.

"Uh, not there Cat-Girl," said a familiar voice. It was Johnnyrotten. "Only cool kids can sit in the back. Animals sit in the front." It seemed the whole back of the bus shook with laughter. Lillie sank into her seat and felt her face get hot. She hated the feeling of aloneness and of being laughed at.

She sighed and got up to head back to the front. As she walked up the aisle, she heard someone call her name.

"Rose!" said Lillie. "But, you weren't on the bus this morning. I thought we were on different busses."

"Only in the morning, I guess. Have a seat!"

The girls talked excitedly about their first day while the bus moved forward. It began rumbling and clattering when it turned onto the brick street of Falls Road. The first stop was at Kenton Road. Lots of kids got off here, including Alexandria and

Johnnyrotten.

Alexandria floated by first, nose in the air, ringlets bouncing with every step. She totally ignored Lillie and Rose. She went down the steps one by one, carefully and slowly, almost as if she intended to slow down the rest of the kids trying to get off the bus.

"There goes the Queen Bee," said Rose.

"And all her royal servants," said Lillie.

"I should have known the two flowers would wind up together," snarled Johnnyrotten as he went by.

"You better watch it, dude, we're the poisonous kind!" said Lillie.

❧   ❧   ❧

Lillie told her dad about what had happened at school that day. She knew she had a big problem. Now not only was Johnnyrotten after her, he thought she had bragged about it and made up stuff.

"It's terrible what you kids go through sometimes," her dad said. "Some kids are just not nice."

"I know."

"Well, when I was a kid I remember there were some other kids who were bigger than me always picking on the littler kids. They never picked on me, though. I don't know what it was. Maybe it was because I was never alone. The bullies tended to pick on kids who were alone a lot of the time. But I usually had a couple of friends with me and we hung out together a lot."

Lillie thought about that. It made sense that one bully wouldn't pick on two or three kids at once. It wouldn't be as easy as picking on just one person. She remembered one boy back at her elementary school in Oregon who liked to sneak up behind girls and yank on their ponytails. His name was Johnny, too. He pulled on her hair once and tried to run away, but not before she pulled on his hair. That was when she was in first grade.

She got in trouble for that and so did he. They had to spend recess together in the principal's office, which was no fun.

She hadn't tried to hurt anyone for any reason since then, and she wasn't about to start now.

She told her mom about her day.

"When I was your age," her mom said, "there were some girls who were my friends. Two of them were my really close friends. Then there was a group of girls who I would never be friends with. It's just how things work."

Lillie thought this made sense, but it still sounded unfair.

"In one of my medical journals I read a theory about development in young girls. They're really figuring out the girl-stuff. They talk about three types of girls- the Alphas, the Betas, and the Gammas.

The Alpha girls are at the top, the ones who tell themselves and everyone else that they are 'popular'. Then the Betas are right behind them, copying whatever the Alphas do. They want to be just like the Alphas, and have the Alphas like them. Have you met any girls like that?"

"Hey, yeah. I have."

"But you-and probably your friend Rose-are the Gammas. You do your own thing and don't really care what other girls think.

"I guess that's us, we're the Gamma Girls!" Lillie said.

"I'm really proud of you sometimes, have I ever told you that?"

"Only every day, Mom," Lillie said, pretending to be annoyed.

10

A Fairy Garden

Lillie yanked off her shoes and tights, grabbed a juice box and a granola bar, and headed outside. She went out the door leading to the overgrown herb garden, and mindlessly walked around the brick patio encircling the thick cluster of plants. The herbs brushed against her bare legs and released their delicate aroma.

She then wandered across the grass and past the pond to the edge of the woods. She saw a path, a deer trail probably, and decided to take it. Lillie wandered along until she came to the top of the hill. She looked down at some old tree stumps, sawed off years ago and painted black to keep them from rotting.

The remains of a campfire from days gone by were partially hidden by years of leaf buildup. Lillie wondered if children had been here and when they had used the fire.

She headed down the hill and sat on a stump across from the old campfire. The silence of the woods and the smells of the approaching autumn washed over her and she was mesmerized.

But suddenly she was jolted back to her senses by noises. Crunching, crashing noises! Someone, something, was walking in the woods from the opposite direction that she had just come from. A bear? She hoped they didn't live in Chagrin Falls. Raccoons...no, they were nocturnal. No rattlesnakes or bob-cats either, but maybe...COYOTES!

Was it a coyote? She had heard a neighbor telling her parents that a few people had spotted coyotes in the woods nearby, down toward the Metroparks. But hadn't they also said that coyotes were skittish, and only ate things 10 pounds and under...

Lillie sat very, very still. She held her breath. She moved her eyes toward the sound and saw, coming out of the bushes and onto the path...Rose!!!!!

"Rose! How did you know I was here?" breathed Lillie as she exhaled.

"I didn't! How did you find this place?" asked Rose. "Did I tell you about this?"

"No, this is the back of *our* property," said Lillie.

"And this is the back of *ours*!" said Rose.

"I didn't realize that Falls Road and Main Street backed up to each other," said Lillie.

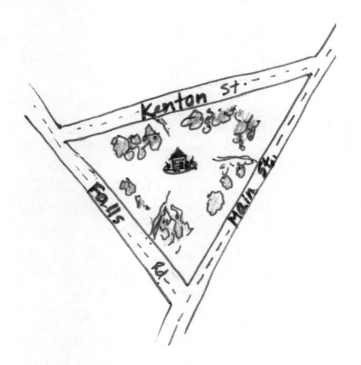

"What a day, huh?" said Rose.

"I told my parents all about Alexandria and Johnnyrotten," said Lillie. "My mom says it sounds like you and I are something called Gamma Girls." She went on to explain the concept to Rose.

"That's us!!" she said. "We are the Gamma Girls of Chagrin Falls!"

❀   ❀   ❀

"I want to show you something," Rose said and she led Lillie down a narrow path through tall grass and bushes.

Finally, they came to a large clearing. There was a small one-room, log cabin that looked like it had been built hundreds of years ago. Surrounding it was a strange circular garden made from all kinds of pinwheels, tiny jingle bells, huge plastic and real flowers, and what looked like a planting of hand mirrors. There were more colors in one place than Lillie had ever seen before.

"This is amazing," Lillie said. "It's all so pretty. Did you do this?"

"It took me a while," Rose said. "But there's a lady in town, Kathleen Gips, and she has a store called The Village Herb Shop and they have all this stuff for a fairy garden."

"A fairy garden?" Lillie asked.

"Sure. All these things are for attracting fairies out of the woods. That plant over there is thyme, which is a fairy's favorite plant. Over there is my mirror garden, because fairies like to look at themselves. They like these little tinkling jingle bells too. When the bells ring, it means the fairies wings have touched them."

"Really? Have you ever seen one?"

"No, not yet. I'm still waiting. They're pretty flighty."

Lillie looked around the garden a little more. Rose had done a lot of work. There were small beds made of moss and little pebble walkways and tiny picket fences. There were acorns turned upside down to catch the morning dew so the fairies could drink.

"What do fairies eat?" Lillie asked.

"Ms. Gips told me that their favorite food is strawberries, and they also like milk and cheese. But I bet they like candy treats too!"

"You want to leave something out for them?"

Rose's eyes got big. "We've got some salt water taffy."

They ran back to Rose's house to get it.

Rose introduced Lillie to her mother, and the girls started talking excitedly to Mrs. Williams about how they had found each other in the woods, and how they were looking for some candy. Mrs. Williams was skeptical when Rose asked her for some. "It's before dinner, Rose," she said. "You can't have candy before dinner."

"But it's not for me, mom. It's for the fairies."

"You and your fairy garden. Do you promise not to eat it yourselves, at least not before dinner?"

"We promise," both Rose and Lillie said.

"Well, all right then. Turn around, the both of you. The candy is kept in a secret place."

"Oh, Mom!" Rose said like she was exasperated. But she turned around, and so did Lillie and they grinned at each other.

Mrs. Williams rattled around all over the kitchen behind them, then handed each of them a bag of wrapped candies from behind. Rose and Lillie smiled at each other, then raced back to the fairy garden.

They set the candy down on a nearby

tree stump.

"Ms. Gips told me that fairies' favorite color is green, so let's pick out the green ones."

The girls looked around for a place to leave the candy. The treats had to be far enough off the ground so that regular animals couldn't get at them but low enough so that the fairies wouldn't have to work very hard to fly up to them.

"What if raccoons get to them?" Lillie asked. "Squirrels could get up here, too. We have to do this right." She bent down over the garden and pulled out a shiny bright lavender ribbon from one of the pinwheels. Then she tied one end of the ribbon to the wax paper of the taffy, and she tied the other end to one of the drooping red branches of a nearby dogwood tree.

"There," she said. "No squirrel or raccoon is going to be able to perch there long
enough to steal it.

"Hey, that's a good idea," Rose said,
genuinely impressed.

"Don't sound so surprised," Lillie
laughed.

They got some more ribbon from the
garden and tied the rest of the taffy to the
dogwood tree.

They sat on the ground for a while, lis-
tening to the wind and watching some
early fall leaves float down to the ground.
Some of the pinwheels spun in the breeze.
The scent of thyme drifted by. The Gamma
Girls were happy.

Sammy's Gone!

Somewhere between Lillie moving to Chagrin Falls and her first day at school, Sammy Calico had disappeared. This had happened before, in Jerome Prairie Valley. Sammy liked to roam. There was no getting around it.

However, it was different for Lillie this time. She did not like losing things anymore. She had never liked losing things, but now that they were away from Oregon, she really hated it.

One morning she spent a half-hour looking for a pencil that she had sharpened the day before. It upset her more than she realized. She did not understand it. There were so many things that she had lost in the fire, and she was not nearly as upset: her silver ring with the six hearts on it, a number of stuffed animals, and a lot of clothes and shoes. They were things she would never see again, but she had gotten used to that.

But things that were lost, things that she might be able to find at any moment, were the worst.

"When was the last time you saw Sammy?" Lillie asked, interrogating her older brother.

"I don't remember," Carter said. "Not since school started. Don't worry about it. He'll come back. He always does."

Her dad was less encouraging. "He's got a whole new world to explore," he said. "He's going to be more curious about his new surroundings here."

Lillie remembered when they got Sammy as a kitten from a neighbor's litter. Each kitten had a different color and pattern. She remembered her mom asking the owner, "Are you sure this is all the same litter?"

❧   ❧   ❧

Lillie and Rose managed to dodge Johnnyrotten and his group the next day in school. Was it because of what Lillie's dad said about not being alone? Whatever it was, Lillie was glad that she didn't have to deal with any bullies.

She did notice, however, that other girls and some of the other boys looked at her differently. Even Alexandria looked at her differently. Maybe it had to do with the colorful ribbons that Lillie and Rose had twirled and braided and tied into their hair while they were hanging up the fairy candy, and maybe it didn't.

One quiet girl came up to her during free time in class and said, "You know, no one's ever stood up to Johnny like that."

"Like what? All I did was trade insults with him. Everybody does that. It doesn't mean anything."

"No one does that with Johnny. I mean no one."

"Well, whatever. Maybe he'll leave me alone now."

"Maybe."

After school, Lillie felt strangely out of breath. Johnnyrotten hadn't done anything to her that day, but who could tell when he would do something? When she got home, she grabbed a water bottle from the refrigerator and took the path to the fairy garden.

Rose was already there, speechless. To their amazement, the candies had been taken and on the ground were the remains of the wax paper wrappers and the ribbons.

Lillie saw Rose's mouth drop open. "I don't believe it!"

"Do you have bears around here?" Lillie asked. It was the first thing she thought of. There were bears in the mountains near Jerome Prairie Valley. It was something you had to remember-you couldn't leave the garbage cans uncovered or else they would get into them.

"Nope. No bears."

"Maybe it's a wolf."

"A wolf wouldn't leave the wrappers on the ground. Neither would anything else."

"Is anything else missing?" Lillie asked.

"I don't think so. I can't believe it! You don't think..."

"No one knows about this but us." Then Lillie laughed. "Us and the fairies!"

Just then the jingle bells started ringing. The girls spun and looked at them in amazement.

"They're here! They want more!" said Rose.

"Hey, let's do it again. Let's put more candy up there," said Lillie.

Lillie and Rose got more candy from Mrs. Bower and more ribbon from the fairy garden.

"Maybe it was Sammy," Lillie said. "He's been missing. He always goes missing. I hope he comes back. He eats a lot, but I'm not so sure he eats candy."

"Of course he'll come back," Rose said. "Cats like being around people. Why don't we look for him? You could show me around your house. I haven't really seen your whole house."

"OK! Let's go!"

The Secret Door

The girls came up on Lillie's house. Lillie showed her around the house, upstairs and around the back. They even went into Lillie's brothers' rooms just in case Sammy Calico had decided to have a nap in one of their closets. They stopped and listened in some of the rooms to see if they could hear a cat mewing or scratching around. But they didn't hear anything.

They looked in the attic, in the barn, and in the closets, but there wasn't a cat anywhere. Then, in the coat closet downstairs,

Lillie thought she heard something.

"It sounds far away," she said.

"It sounds like wind," Rose said. They looked at each other, then they started pulling out all of the coats and the boots and the umbrellas. But there was nothing there.

Rose walked into the closet and crouched down on the floor. "I feel something," she said. "Something underneath my feet."

Rose stepped aside and started pulling up the rug.

"Hey!" Lillie said. "What are you..." Then she stopped. Her eyes got wide and her mouth opened.

Rose peeled back the rug from the floor to reveal a trap door in the floorboards. The handle was sunken so it wouldn't poke up through the carpet.

"Wow!" Lillie said.

There was a draft coming from the edges of the door, and they could hear wind noises coming through. Rose tried to pull it open, but it wouldn't move. She knocked on it.

"I think it's hollow," she said. "You've

got a secret passageway underneath your house!"

Lillie grabbed hold of the handle and pulled. "Help me, Rose!" she said. They pulled together.

Finally, it creaked a little. Then it came up about six inches. They pulled harder and it slipped away with loud pops and cracks.

"I think we just broke the house!" Rose said.

They all looked at the splintered remains of the closet floor. The trap door had come up and off, but not without taking a good part of the floor with it.

"Oops! That looks like two days' worth of work to fix," Lillie said. "For Dad," she added.

"What's that smell?" Rose asked.

There was a funny smell coming from the new opening in the floor. It was like old oranges.

"There's only one way to find out," Lillie said. "This could be an adventure. The Gamma Girls need to make a plan."

The girls talked and came up with a list of things they would need. Lillie then ran

upstairs to get them. She returned with flashlights, a chair, and some old pillows. They
lowered the chair into the hole until it was
steady, then tossed the pillows down around
it in case anyone fell.

Lillie went down first, slowly inching
herself backwards while on her stomach.
When her dangling feet felt the seat of the
chair, she let the rest of her body slide in.
Rose held tight onto Lillie's arms until her
friend was safe.

When they were both down, they shined
their flashlights in different directions. The
floor was dirt, packed hard like cement, but
cold and damp. There were many rooms and
tunnels underneath the house, with thick
wood beams coming up out of the ground to
support the first floor.

"Let's try this way," Rose said. She
shined her flashlight down a long hallway

that connected to a small room. They followed the beam of light and went through the doorway into the chamber.

Lillie's flashlight passed over something on the ground that made her jump.

"OH!" she yelled.

"What is it?" Rose asked.

Lillie tried to find it again. Rose helped. Then she found it and jumped. "Whoa!" she said suddenly.

It was the skeleton of a small animal.

❁   ❁   ❁

"Poor Sammy." Lillie breathed out quietly and slowly.

"Oh Lillie," was all Rose could manage.

The girls stood next to each other, quiet and unmoving.

Lillie broke the silence. "Wait a minute. I wonder how long this has been here?" she said as she kneeled down by it. "This can't be Sammy. He's probably only been gone about a week, so he wouldn't be a skeleton yet. This skeleton could be from last year, or it could be from twenty years ago. It's probably a squirrel or a small raccoon or possum."

"Hey, look!" Rose said. Her flashlight was all the way across the room. Lillie went over.

"There's a small opening here. It looks like this is underneath your back porch."

Lillie could see it now. The opening was behind a supporting beam where they could see daylight shining through the cracks.

"That's just big enough for a cat to fit through," Lillie said. "I wonder if Sammy's been here."

As the girls got closer, they noticed a tiny pinprick of gleaming that poked out of the floor. Lillie bent down to scratch at it with her fingers while Rose held the light directly on it.

"It's a ring," Lillie whispered. She scratched away more of the dirt that covered it. "A silver ring."

She slid it onto her finger.

"Very cool!" said Rose. "I wonder who lost it?"

The girls left the little room and the skeleton and went back to the entrance.

Rose ran her light against the wall, back and forth. "You know, this would be a pretty great place to have a clubhouse."

"I didn't even know this was here," Lillie said. "My mom didn't say anything about this. I wonder if we could make this into a real basement!"

13

The Silver Ring

By that evening, the Jecmens and Rose had done a lot of cleaning down in the basement. Lillie and Rose had brought down some old rugs, some blankets and a couple of soft beanbag chairs. Mr. Jecmen managed to hang up a light bulb on the end of a long, orange extension cord that was plugged in upstairs.

It was agreed that the trap door had to remain open at all times so Sammy could see the light and find his way out.

Dad propped a ladder against the opening, but the chair remained there as well, just in case Sammy needed a launching pad to jump out of the room. They also put Sammy's food and water dishes in the basement and made sure they were always full.

Carter protested that Lillie got to use the room. "I'm the oldest," he said. "It should be mine."

"Lillie found it," Dad said. "Besides, she was the only one looking for Sammy."

Lillie and Rose sat in the clubhouse and listened to Lillie's family discuss the basement from the floor above. Lillie's mom said it was probably just a root cellar that no one ever did anything with. It was used to store apples when the property had an orchard on it over a hundred years ago. She guessed that somewhere along the line, someone just covered up the opening with new flooring and everyone forgot about it.

"I don't even remember anything like this," she said.

The girls were looking carefully along the walls to see if they could find something interesting. Their flashlights moved slowly along the stone walls. They hoped to find more secret passageways and chambers.

"You know my parents are divorced," Rose said.

"Yeah," Lillie said. "You said that once."

"It's not as bad as it sounds. I live with my mom, but my dad and I get along fine. I just wish I could see them both every day, you know?"

The voices in the house above faded away, and it was very quiet. It was as if the sounds of the world had run off and hidden in a rabbit hole.

Then they thought they heard a very soft mewing sound. Lillie sprang up and ran to the small opening they had found earlier.

Nothing was around.

"That had to have been Sammy," she said in the darkness. "Something's been eating the food out of his bowl, but I haven't seen him."

"Don't worry. You know he's OK, and he'll be back soon."

"I know. But I just like him to stay around."

Lillie's mom stuck her head down into the hole, "I think it's time for you two to come up above ground. Rose, your mom said you could stay for dinner if you like. We're having spaghetti."

"Sure!"

• • •

Lillie's mom had left the ring to soak in some warm, soapy water. After dinner, she finished washing off the red clay and dirt from the ring with an old toothbrush.

"Well, I'll be!" she said. "Everyone, come look at this!"

Mrs. Jecmen handed the ring carefully to Lillie and pointed to the inside. There, in the tiniest letters imaginable, only as wide as a straight pin, were the letters L-I-L-L-I-E.

"This must have been your great-grandmother's ring. You were named after her, Lillie. She and your great-grandfather built this house."

"Wow!" said Lillie. "I wonder when she lost it?"

"Probably when she was down in the root cellar sorting all those apples. I hear she ran that orchard business from top to bottom. She was a Gamma Girl before her time. You've got it in your genes, Lillie!"

The next afternoon, Lillie and Rose had found that more of the candy from their fairy garden was missing. But this time, whatever it was also took the wrappers with them and left the ribbons on the ground.

14

A Gamma Plan

Something strange happened at the school the next day. A few of the girls in the fourth grade wore the same kinds of ribbons in their hair that Lillie and Rose had worn the day before.

Neither Lillie nor Rose had thought to put the ribbons in their hair that morning—it was just a one-time thing as far as they were concerned. But Lillie counted at least ten girls who were doing it.

"Even Marietta!" Rose said at lunchtime. "But not Alexandria!" she giggled.

That was when Alexandria came up to them. "Hey guys," she said, trying to sound friendly. Her blond hair was ribbon-free and tied back in the pony-tail.

"Yes?" Lillie said.

"You two have turned into quite the trend-setters."

Rose laughed nervously.

"We can't wait to see what you're going to do next. Oh, but you didn't wear your ribbons today, did you?"

Then Alexandria pulled out a couple of beautiful shiny ribbons from her pocket. They were metallic colors that glinted in the sunlight.

In front of both of them, Alexandria took her hair out of the pony-tail and tied the metallic ribbons into it like she had been doing it her whole life. Her hair looked like it was made for those ribbons.

Then Alexandria waved a little wave with just her fingers. "Ta-ta, girls," she said with a fake smile as she skipped away toward a few of her friends.

"What was all that about?" Lillie asked.

"She thinks she's so superior," Rose said.

Just as lunch was ending, both Lillie and Rose were stopped in the hallway by Johnnyrotten, who jumped out from behind a corner.

"Hello ladies," he said smugly. "I wanted to thank you for all the candy."

"Huh?" both girls said.

"That was some of the best salt water taffy I've ever had!" he chortled as he passed them by. Then he threw the empty green wrappers to the ground and headed back to class, turning his back on them and laughing.

"That rotten..." Rose began.

"That no-good..." Lillie started.

They looked at each other, and then sighed. As they went back to class, they threw away the wrappers they had picked up.

"Now we know that he knows where the fairy garden is," Lillie said. "At least he hasn't done anything to that."

"He wouldn't dare," Rose said.

"Yes he would. So, we have to make sure he doesn't. Meet at the fairy garden. The Gamma Girls need a plan."

They gave each other high fives and then

went to their separate classrooms.

❧   ❧   ❧

After school, Rose and Lillie ran to the garden from their houses with their snacks.

"What can we do to him?" Rose asked.

Lillie was so mad, she couldn't think straight. She still couldn't believe that he had taken their candy.

"We could start a rumor about him," Rose said.

"That would be really mean," Lillie said, grinning. She started to imagine the shocked faces of other kids when she told them something about him. But then she calmed down and thought about it. "That's not exactly kind."

"*Kind?*" Rose asked. "What do you mean by 'kind'? He ate our candy. Then he shoved it in our faces, remember? That wasn't kind at all. We have to get him back, don't we?"

Lillie thought about that for a moment. "We can't just let him get away with it. But we can't be mean like he is. It's not the Gamma way. Maybe we don't have to get him back. I mean, what if we make him really mad and he does something worse."

"He would. But we have to do something," Rose said. "Maybe if we don't do something to him, we can at least keep him away from here."

"What are you thinking, Rose?"

"Even if Johnnyrotten doesn't come back, one of his friends might. We have to boy-proof this garden."

"Hey, yeah! We can put up signs. Set traps. Dig a pit and put branches over it..."

Rose picked up some soil and rubbed it between her fingers.

"I was thinking we could hang more candy, but this time put a little surprise in each one. Like we can mix dirt in with the taffy, or sand..."

"Or hot sauce!"

Rose snapped her fingers. "I've got it! Is that skeleton still there?"

"I think so."

"I know of a way we can use it to keep people away," said Rose.

Six Little Surprises!

The two girls ran back to Lillie's house. They went right to the trap door to the basement and inched down the ladder, pointing their flashlights into the darkness. They followed the beam of light that led them through the rooms and doorways, and down the halls and passages.

"There it is," Rose said, shining her light on the brightness of the skeleton.

"This will look great next to a sign at the fairy garden that says 'Beware! Rabid Skunk Nest'!" said Lillie.

Lillie was about to pick it up when they heard a noise, somewhere between a squeak and a wheeze. Lillie froze in her tracks. She shined her light in the direction of the sound. The girls walked quickly but quietly down the long hall and into their clubhouse.

There, on a nest of the pillows that Lillie and Rose had brought down with them the day before, was Sammy, with six kittens all snuggled together. Sammy licked them while purring loudly and proudly. One large front paw covered the babies protectively and gently.

"What...?" Lillie started to ask.

"I thought you said Sammy was a boy cat!" Rose said.

The kittens were crawling around each other along Sammy's belly. Sammy looked relaxed, if not completely comfortable.

"I thought he was. She was. She used to be!"

Lillie ran up the ladder and shouted, "Dad! Come quick!"

Lillie's dad came down the ladder with a heavy-duty flashlight. "Well, I'll be," he said. "So that's where Sammy's been. I have to call your mother." He went back up the ladder.

"I can't believe Sammy was a girl this whole time and we didn't know!" Lillie said.

"Is it OK to pick up the kittens?" Rose asked.

"Not yet," Lillie said. "The mom might reject them if they smell like us. Or she might hide them somewhere else to protect them. In about a week, we can start to hold them."

The kittens were very tiny, less than a full day old. Their eyes hadn't opened yet, and they looked like little bean bag toys-the kind that were shaped like a cat and put on the end of a key-chain!

Lillie gently pointed to them, one by one, calling out the colors.

"A calico," she whispered. "An orange tabby... A gray one... A white one... A white one with two black dots... A black and grey tiger stripe..."

Lillie's dad came back down. He was still on the phone. "We all thought so," her dad said into the phone. "No, I'm looking at them right now... Yes, I'm sure they're Sammy's... OK. OK. I'll tell them."

He closed the phone and put it in his pocket. Rose scratched Sammy's head as Lillie followed the kittens' movements.

"So, *he*..." Lillie's dad started to say. "I mean, *she* was pregnant. That's why she was so fat when we left Oregon. We thought it was because she was eating at two different families."

"That's *why* she was eating at two different families! Can we still call her Sammy?" Lillie asked.

"I don't see why not. Samantha is a fine name for a mama cat," her dad said.

"We should have had her fixed before

we left Oregon," he said. "We just left in such a rush... I called the vet here to make an appointment and when I told her about our male calico, she said calicos are almost always female."

"Why does Sammy need to be fixed?" Lillie asked. "Is she broken?"

Dad laughed. "No, Lillie-belle. We just need to take her to the vet to make sure that she doesn't have any more kittens. We can't keep all these kittens as it is."

"I guess that's true."

"What are you going to do with all of them?" Rose asked.

"We need to find good homes for them," Dad said. "It would be way too expensive to keep so many cats."

"But we can still keep Sammy, can't we?" Lillie asked.

"Of course."

Sammy purred underneath Rose's hand. And as Lillie and Rose looked into the tiny faces of those helpless, mewling kittens, they forgot all about everything outside that room, including Johnnyrotten and Alexandria.

Lillie's first week at her new school was over, but her adventures in Chagrin Falls were just beginning.

The End

♣   ♣   ♣

Oh, no! Alexandria is insisting that she gets to have one of Lillie's kittens! What will the Gamma Girls do?

Find out in Book #2 of The Gamma Girls of Chagrin Falls!

♣   ♣   ♣

Janet Kuivila has a Master's Degree in Social Work and a Ph.D. in Psychology. She was a therapist for many years before taking time off to write and raise her family. Originally from Oregon, she now lives in an 1850's farmhouse in Chagrin Falls, Ohio with her husband, their three children, and numerous cats and dogs.

Jane McKelvey, M.A., A.T., practices art therapy at a couseling center outside of Cleveland, Ohio specializing in child art therapy. She utilizes the healing properties of the creative process in her work and in her life. Jane and Matt live in a century home in Chagrin Falls, Ohio with her daughter, Bradley, their cat, Fiona, and their dog, Blue.

Please contact us at
www.LillieandRose.com